This
Ladybird book
belongs to

....

Published by Ladybird Books Ltd
A Penguin Company
Penguin Books Ltd, 80 Strand, London WC2R 0RL, UK
Penguin Books Australia Ltd, 707 Collins Street, Melbourne, Victoria 3008, Australia
Penguin Group (NZ) 67 Apollo Drive, Rosedale, North Shore 0632, New Zealand

001

© Ladybird Books Limited MMXIII

Text © Judith Nicholls MMIII

ISBN: 978-0-72327-154-3

Printed in China

Ladybird
I'm Ready...to Read!
Snick-Snack Sniffle-Nose

written by Judith Nicholls ★ illustrated by Emilie Chollat

"Stop!" said the Snick-Snack Sniffle-Nose Clip-Clop Troll.

"This is my log! Stop there on the grass.
I won't let you pass!"

"Let me pass," said the Flip-Flop Frog.
"This is my pond! Let me pass,
or I'll hop on your log!"

"Hop!" said the Snick-Snack Sniffle-Nose Clip-Clop Troll.

"You can hop, you can plop,
you can flip, you can flop,
but this is my log. I won't let you pass!"

"Let me pass!" said the plump old rat.
"This is my pond. Let me pass,
or I'll jump on your hat!"

13

"Jump!" said the Snick-Snack Sniffle-Nose Clip-Clop Troll.

"You can jump, you can clump,
you can bump, you can thump,
but this is my log. I won't let you pass!"

"Let me pass," said the cold old wind
from the end of the pond.

"This is my pond! Let me pass,
or I'll huff and I'll puff,
and I'll blow your big log
to the end of the land."

17

"Huff!" said the Snick-Snack Sniffle-Nose Clip-Clop Troll.

"You can huff, you can puff,
you can puff, you can huff,
but this is my log. I won't let you pass!"

The cold old wind from the end of the pond was cross.

"I am the boss!" he said to the Snick-Snack Sniffle-Nose Clip-Clop Troll.

"Hop!" said the wind to the Flip-Flop Frog.

"Jump!" said the wind to the plump old rat.

Then he huffed and he puffed, and he puffed, and he huffed...

"HUFF!"

25

...and he blew the Snick-Snack Sniffle-Nose Clip-Clop Troll to the end of the land.

"STOP!"

And the Snick-Snack Sniffle-Nose
Clip-Clop Troll was never seen again.

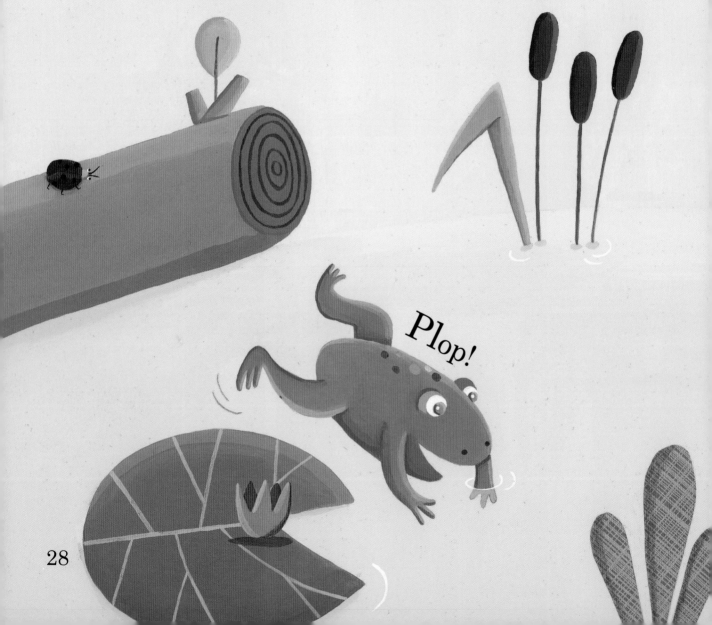

Plop!

29